LIBRARY OF DOOM

THE FINAL CHAPTERS

TOME RAIDER

By Michael Dahl

Illustrated by
Nelson Evergreen

raintree
a Capstone company — publishers for children

Raintree is an imprint of Capstone Global Library Limited, a company incorporated in England and Wales having its registered office at 7 Pilgrim Street, London, EC4V 6LB – Registered company number: 6695582

www.raintree.co.uk
myorders@raintree.co.uk

Designed by Hilary Wacholz
Printed and bound in China by Nordica
0914/CA21401556
ISBN 978-1-4062-9451-4
19 18 17 16 15
10 9 8 7 6 5 4 3 2 1

British Library Cataloguing in Publication Data
A full catalogue record for this book is available from the British Library.

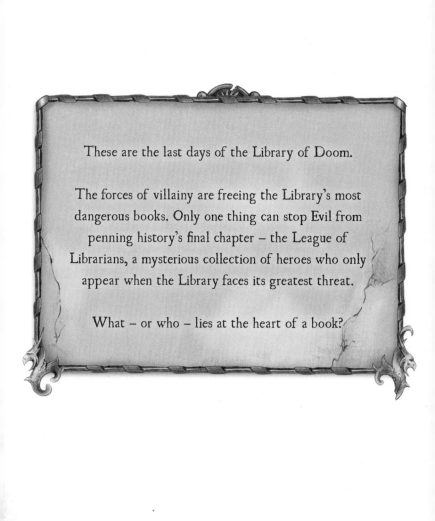

These are the last days of the Library of Doom.

The forces of villainy are freeing the Library's most dangerous books. Only one thing can stop Evil from penning history's final chapter – the League of Librarians, a mysterious collection of heroes who only appear when the Library faces its greatest threat.

What – or who – lies at the heart of a book?

TABLE OF CONTENTS

Chapter 1

THE TOMES

Six GIANT slabs stand silently in the desert.

This desert is no ordinary desert.

It is a vast cavern hidden **deep** within the Library of Doom.

The slabs are no ordinary rock formations.

They are gigantic books made of metal. They are the fabled Tomes of Oom.

A figure lands on the windy top of the first Tome.

It is the Iron Page.

His metal armour is dark as ink. A visor of black diamond covers his face.

The Iron Page scans the rooftop of the Tome.

He has never been here before.

He is **alone**.

Then he hears a voice.

Another figure has landed nearby.

"Iron!" cries the new arrival.

It is the **Librarian**.

He is the head guardian of the Library of Doom.

"You summoned me, sir?" says the figure in armour.

The Librarian nods.

"A thief is after the Vowel Stones," he says. "If we do not stop him, the Library of Doom will **fall**!"

Chapter 2

THE FIRST TRAP

"A Vowel Stone is locked deep within each Tome," says the Librarian.

"Each gem holds a terrible power," he adds. "If the Stones are lost or stolen, the Library of Doom will vanish."

And we will vanish too, the Iron Page tells himself. *All of our power comes from the Vowel Stones.*

"We will find the thief," says the Iron Page.

The Librarian smiles grimly. "The Tomes are full of traps," he says.

Then the Librarian turns and leads his companion to the edge of the roof.

A narrow set of rusty metal stairs angles down the face of the Tome.

As the two guardians **descend** the stairs, a fierce wind surrounds them.

"It is the Breath," shouts the Librarian. "One of the traps."

The wind grows stronger.

The two guardians cling to the wall of the metal slab.

In the powerful wind, it is **impossible** for them to move.

The Iron Page almost loses his balance.

The steps are **sliding back** into the wall of the Tome.

Soon there will be nothing left for the librarians to stand on.

"**Hurry!**" shouts the Librarian.

The two men run down the steps.

"Wait!" cries the Iron Page.

He rubs his gloves together, faster and faster.

His arms and hands become a dark blur.

"Quickly, give me your hand!" the Iron Page says.

The **Librarian** grabs the iron glove of his companion.

The stairs beneath their feet slide all the way inside the wall. But the two guardians do not fall.

Iron has **magnetized** himself.

His armour clings tightly to the metal wall.

Chapter 3

THE SECOND GEM

The two companions `slide` along the wall.

They make their way to a small window.

They climb through the window and find themselves in a **dark hall**.

"I know the way to the Stone," says the Librarian.

They move closer to the heart of the Tome.

Then a **low rumble** echoes through the empty halls.

"It's another trap," says the Librarian. "The Vibration."

The metal walls and floor **shiver** like an earthquake.

The two men are thrown onto the floor. They cannot move or walk.

The Iron Page rubs his gloves together in the other direction.

His armour is magnetized in a new way.

It pushes against the metal hallway and floor.

He **rises** into the air, holding on to the other Librarian.

They float through the halls, without touching the building around them.

Soon, two **tall doors** open in front of them.

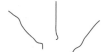

A brilliant yellow **light** greets them as they enter a wide chamber.

At the centre of the chamber, a giant metal skull hangs above the floor.

Inside the skull glows a yellow gem.

It is the size of a human head.

Iron has never seen a Vowel Stone before. "It's beautiful," he says.

"And it's mine!" says the Librarian.

Chapter 4

I FOR I

The Librarian pulls another gem from his pack.

The new one **glows** bright blue.

"I already stole this one from the third Tome," cries the Librarian.

He holds up the brilliant blue gem.

"This is the I Stone," he says. "And with its power, I can become whoever I wish."

"But how?" says Iron.

The air around the Librarian ripples like a mirage. His face and body change shape.

It is not the Librarian.

It is the Grim Reader, the sworn enemy of the Library of Doom.

"I knew when I took the first Stone, all the traps would be activated," says the Reader. "That's why I pretended to be the Librarian. I knew your powers would help me enter this Tome. And now that I have two of the gems, nothing can stop me!"

Iron bows his head. *All of our power comes from the Vowel Stones*, he tells himself.

The Iron Page quickly removes his diamond visor.

He **throws** it at the Reader's hands, and it rushes through the air.

The hard diamond slices through the Vowel Stones.

The Vowels are doubled and fall to the floor.

Suddenly, a weird pulsing sound fills the air.

The Grim Reader cries out and claps his hands to his ears.

The Vowel sounds vibrate through the room.

The metal skull hanging in the middle of the chamber begins to shudder. It swings and sways.

It falls towards the Reader, trapping him within its metal jaws.

The Iron Page snatches up the cut gems.

His magnetic gloves force the **broken** pieces together.

Then he turns to the fallen and bruised Reader.

"No more doubles, no more copies," says the Iron Page. "I'm taking you back to the real Librarian. The one and only."

GLOSSARY

activated – turned on or put into action

gem – precious stone

magnetized – made a piece of magnetic material and able to attract iron or steel

mirage – something that you think you see in the distance that is not really there

page – young person who works as a helper or as a servant for someone

pulsing – beating or throbbing steadily

tome – book, especially a big and heavy one, or one volume from a larger work

vast – very large in size or amount

vibrate – move back and forth quickly and repeatedly

DISCUSSION QUESTIONS

1. The giant books called the Tomes have powers deep inside them. Do you think that real books have powers? Explain your answer.

2. The Iron Page comes to help as soon as he is summoned. He shows courage and loyalty. Are there people you are loyal to? Are there people who are loyal to you?

3. Why do you think the Grim Reader pretended to be the Librarian to steal the Stones? Why would he turn against the Library?

WRITING PROMPTS

1. Two of the traps that protect the Tomes are called the Breath and the Vibration. What do you think the other traps are? Write a description of what they are and how they work.

2. This story shows two of the powerful Vowel Stones. Write a paragraph telling what the other Stones are like and what their powers are.

3. The hero in this book is the Iron Page. If you were one of the guardians of the Library of Doom, what would your uniform be like? How would it help you protect the Library?

THE AUTHOR

Michael Dahl is the prolific author of the bestselling *Goodnight, Baseball* picture book and more than 200 other books for children and young adults. He has won the AEP Distinguished Achievement Award three times for his non-fiction, a Teachers' Choice Award from *Learning* magazine and a Seal of Excellence from the Creative Child Awards. He is also the author of the Hocus Pocus Hotel mysteries and the Dragonblood series. Dahl currently lives in Minneapolis, Minnesota, USA.

THE ILLUSTRATOR

Nelson Evergreen lives on the south coast of England with his partner and their imaginary cat. Evergreen is a comics artist, illustrator and general all-round doodler of whatever nonsense pops into his head. He contributes regularly to the UK underground comics scene, and is currently writing and illustrating a number of graphic novel and picture book hybrids for older children.